Arctic Ocean

Europe

Asia

Tethys Ocean

Africa

India

Australia

Antarctica

This book belongs to:

For Peter and Sophie

Neffy and the Feathered Dinosaurs is © Flying Eye Books 2016.

This is a first edition published in 2016 by Flying Eye Books, an imprint of
Nobrow Ltd. 62 Great Eastern Street, London, EC2A 3QR.

Text and illustrations © Joe Lillington 2016.
Joe Lillington has asserted his right under the Copyright, Designs and
Patents Act, 1988, to be identified as the Author and Illustrator of this Work.

Published in the US by Nobrow (US) Inc.
Printed in Turkey on FSC assured paper.

ISBN 978-1-909263-89-5
Order from www.flyingeyebooks.com

Neffy
and the
Feathered Dinosaurs
By Joe Lillington

FLYING EYE BOOKS
London • New York

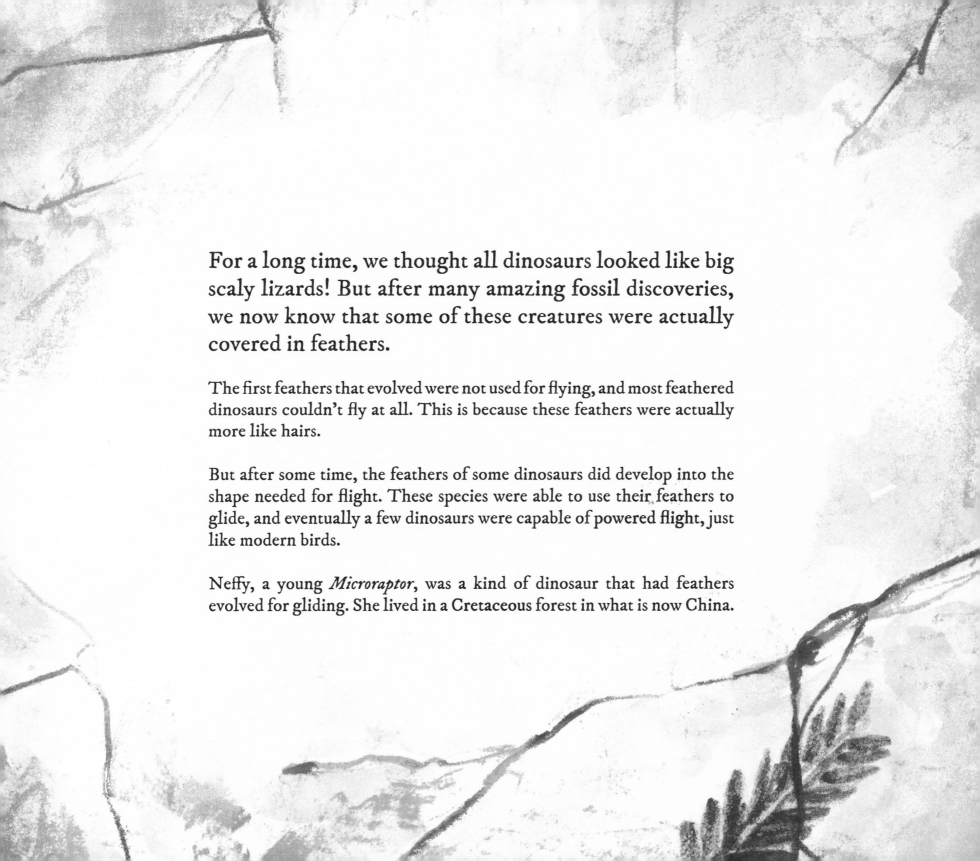

For a long time, we thought all dinosaurs looked like big scaly lizards! But after many amazing fossil discoveries, we now know that some of these creatures were actually covered in feathers.

The first feathers that evolved were not used for flying, and most feathered dinosaurs couldn't fly at all. This is because these feathers were actually more like hairs.

But after some time, the feathers of some dinosaurs did develop into the shape needed for flight. These species were able to use their feathers to glide, and eventually a few dinosaurs were capable of powered flight, just like modern birds.

Neffy, a young *Microraptor*, was a kind of dinosaur that had feathers evolved for gliding. She lived in a Cretaceous forest in what is now China.

It was a very special day for Neffy.
She would be taking her first flight.

"Come on Neffy, it's easy!"
called her sisters as they flew ahead.
They made it look so simple...

Microraptor
Microraptor gui

Weight	Up to 1 kg
Size	Up to 0.7 m long
Diet	Carnivore
Habitat	Forest
Family	Dromaeosauridae
Location	China
Lived	Early Cretaceous, 125 MYA

Even though *Microraptor* had four wings, it wasn't capable of powered flight. Instead, it was very good at gliding, using all four of its wings and its large feathered tail to soar through the air.

By comparing the arrangement and shape of cells in the feathers of fossilised *Microraptor* to those found in modern birds, palaeontologists discovered that their feathers would have been an iridescent black colour.

But when Neffy spread her wings she didn't know what she was supposed to do!
Scared of being left behind, she took her first nervous step off the branch and...

Uhoh!

"What are you doing!
You almost crushed me!"
shrieked a little sinosauropteryx.

crash!

"Sorry..." Neffy whimpered,
looking back up at the sky.

Sinosauropteryx
Sinosauropteryx prima

Weight	Up to 0.5 kg
Size	Up to 1.2 m long
Diet	Carnivore
Habitat	Temperate forest
Family	Compsognathidae
Location	China
Lived	Early Cretaceous, 125 MYA

A fossilised *Sinosauropteryx* was found with its last meal, the fossilised remains of a small mammal, still present in its stomach!

Sinosauropteryx had a really long tail. It was the longest tail compared to the size of its body of any theropod.

She quickly ran across the forest floor after her sisters. But soon they were too high and too far away.

Troodon
Troodon formosus

Weight	Up to 50 kg
Size	Up to 2.4 m long
Diet	Carnivore or omnivore
Habitat	Across North America
Family	Troodontidae
Location	North America
Lived	Late Cretaceous, 77 MYA

Many *Troodon* nests have been found. The female would lay her eggs in pairs, until there were around 24 in the nest. Laying quickly meant the eggs would all hatch around the same time. When she was finished, the male would brood over the eggs until they hatched.

Troodon had large forward-facing eyes, giving it good vision for hunting, even at night. Palaeontologists think they might have been **nocturnal** hunters.

All alone, she ran even faster until she came to a forest clearing.

"Can you teach me how to fly?" she asked the first dinosaur she saw.

"I don't know how to fly!" replied the gallimimus.

"But I did see some flying dinosaurs headed that way," she pointed.

Gallimimus
Gallimimus bullatus

Weight	Up to 440 kg	
Size	Up to 8 m long	
Diet	Herbivore or omnivore	
Habitat	Open woodland	
Family	Ornithomimidae	
Location	Mongolia	
Lived	Late Cretaceous, 70 MYA	

Various adaptations, such as long legs and a thick counterbalancing tail, suggest that *Gallimimus* would have been a very fast runner.

Gallimimus had a thin beak for its mouth instead of a toothed jaw. The beak was only a few millimetres thick in some places!

As Neffy hurried along she spotted another dinosaur among the leaves. "You've got lots of feathers, can you fly?" Neffy asked, but there was no reply.

The nothronychus was too busy stuffing his face!
"I think you're too big to fly anyway..."
Neffy mumbled, as she squeezed past.

Nothronychus
Nothronychus mckinleyi

Weight	Up to 900 kg
Size	Up to 6 m long
Diet	Herbivore
Habitat	Tropical jungle
Family	Therizinosauridae
Location	North America
Lived	Late Cretaceous, 91 MYA

Nothronychus was a strange looking dinosaur. As well as its long thin claws, it had a large pot belly, a long neck and arms, and leaf-shaped teeth!

Even though *Nothronychus* was a herbivore, it actually evolved from **carnivores** and is related to the mighty predator *Tyrannosaurus rex*.

"Such beautiful feathers!
He must be able to fly!" thought
Neffy, but he couldn't.

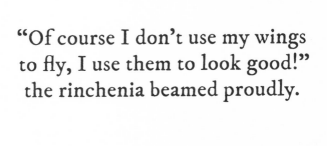

"Of course I don't use my wings to fly, I use them to look good!" the rinchenia beamed proudly.

"I know all about flying!" called an excited voice. "My name is Poros, follow me!"

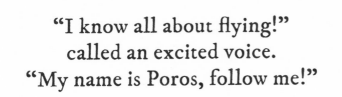

Rinchenia
Rinchenia mongoliensis

Weight	Up to 136 kg
Size	Up to 2.5 m long
Diet	Omnivore
Habitat	Woodland and plains
Family	Oviraptoridae
Location	Mongolia
Lived	Late Cretaceous, 70 MYA

Rinchenia was a kind of oviraptor. Fossilised oviraptors have been found brooding over egg clutches, just like modern day birds sitting on their nests.

Rinchenia's tail bones were similar to the ones in modern birds. This means that it would have been able to lift its tail feathers and shake them like a peacock.

"Can you really fly?"
Neffy warily asked the buitreraptor.

"Well, no, but I understand how it's done!"
laughed Poros, as he showed her
how to flap her wings.

Buitreraptor
Buitreraptor gonzalezorum

Weight	Up to 3 kg
Size	Up to 1.5 m long
Diet	Carnivore
Habitat	Woodland and plains
Family	Dromaeosauridae
Location	Argentina
Lived	Late Cretaceous, 90 MYA

It has not been confirmed whether *Buitreraptor* had feathers or not; however, many related dinosaurs did, so it is assumed they did too.

Buitreraptor was a piscivore and had a long thin snout, which would have helped it reach out and snap up its slippery little prey.

Neffy and Poros were so
busy practicing that they didn't realize
they were being watched by a
hungry pack of deinonychus...

crash!

"Run, Neffy!"
shouted Poros.

Snap!

Deinonychus
Deinonychus antirrhopus

Weight	Up to 70 kg
Size	Up to 3.4 m long
Diet	Carnivore
Habitat	Tropical forest
Family	Dromaeosauridae
Location	North America
Lived	Early Cretaceous, 110 MYA

Many palaeontologists believe *Deinonychus* would have hunted as a pack to bring down large prey that they would not have been able to tackle alone.

It is believed that *Deinonychus* used its strong curved toe claw to hold down prey and eat them alive, like modern birds of prey.

Neffy was falling again, but this time
she knew what to do. She held out her wings
like her friend had shown her and...

"Phew! A lucky escape,"
she thought. Then she realised,
"I'm really doing it! I'm flying!"

Whoosh!

She soared higher and higher.
"Can you teach me how you loop like that?"
she asked a passing flock of confuciusornis.

The confuciusornis swooped over to show Neffy what to do when suddenly...

Confuciusornis
Confuciusornis sanctus

Weight	Up to 1.5 kg
Size	Up to 0.7 m long
Diet	Omnivore
Habitat	Woodland and lakes
Family	Confuciusornithidae
Location	China
Lived	Early Cretaceous, 120 MYA

Confuciusornis would have looked very similar to modern birds, with fully developed feathers and males with long tail feathers for display.

They were very common and were good fliers, living in large flocks. A flock of 40 were discovered close together, possibly killed by volcanic ash or gas.

"Coming through!" thundered an enormous pteranodon, as it streaked through the flock.

"Hey!" squawked a disgruntled Neffy.
"Pterosaurs are so rude!"
clucked the confuciusornis.

Pteranodon
Pteranodon longiceps

Weight	Between 20–90 kg
Size	Up to 7 m wingspan
Diet	Piscivore
Habitat	Woodland and lakes
Family	Pteranodontidae
Location	North America
Lived	Late Cretaceous, 85 MYA

Though *Pteranodon* and other pterosaurs like it are sometimes portrayed to look similar to dinosaurs and did live at the same time, pterosaurs were not dinosaurs. They were reptiles that evolved flight independently.

Pterosaurs did not have feathers like the feathered dinosaurs either. Instead they were covered in things similar to hairs, called pycnofibres, which palaeontologists think kept them warm, just like fur would.

The sky was a busy place. Neffy wasn't the only one who could fly! As she swooped down to land, she saw her sisters at last and heard a familiar voice call out...

"You did it, Neffy!"

Tyrannosaurus
Tyrannosaurus rex

Weight	Up to 6800 kg
Size	Up to 12.3 m long
Diet	Carnivore
Habitat	Plains and forests
Family	Tyrannosauridae
Location	North America
Lived	Late Cretaceous, 66 MYA

Tyrannosaurus rex was once thought to be the largest predatory dinosaur, but since then even larger species have been found! However, it is still thought to have had the most powerful bite of any animal that has ever lived.

It is uncertain whether *Tyrannosaurus rex* had feathers; however, many palaeontologists now believe its young were covered in a layer of soft feathers for warmth. The amount of feathers they had might have changed over time depending on the environment they lived in.

In the end, it wasn't the biggest or the most fearsome dinosaurs that survived extinction.

It was small feathered dinosaurs like Neffy, who were more adaptable to changes in their environment and whose descendants eventually evolved into modern day birds.

How big were they?

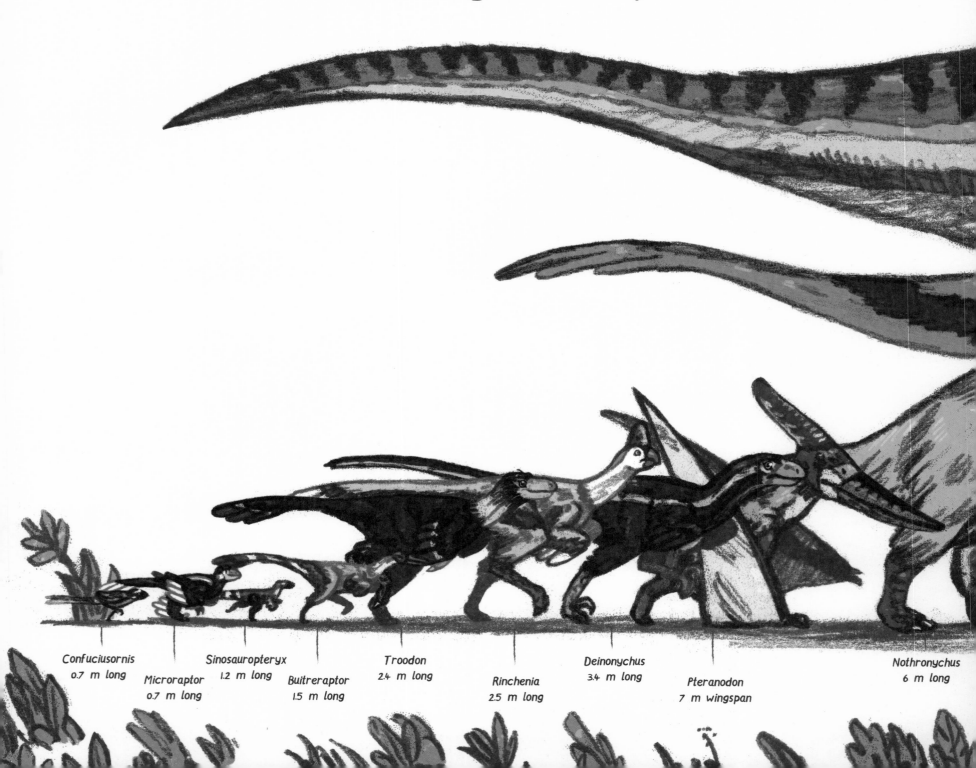

Confuciusornis
0.7 m long

Microraptor
0.7 m long

Sinosauropteryx
1.2 m long

Buitreraptor
1.5 m long

Troodon
2.4 m long

Rinchenia
2.5 m long

Deinonychus
3.4 m long

Pteranodon
7 m wingspan

Nothronychus
6 m long

Gallimimus
8 m long

Tyrannosaurus
12.3 m long

AUTHOR'S NOTE

In reality it would have been impossible for Neffy to meet all the dinosaurs she has in this story, since many lived in different times and places.

Neffy's journey has been told in this way so you can enjoy the story and learn about other feathered dinosaurs at the same time. To find out where and when each dinosaur lived, you can refer to the map at the end of the book and the facts on each page.

Palaeontologists are still making new discoveries about feathered dinosaurs all the time, so what we think about how they lived can change as we learn more about them.

Neffy's and Poros' names are from Ancient Greek mythology. Neffy is named after Nephele, a cloud nymph, and Poros was the name of the spirit of resourcefulness.

GLOSSARY

Carnivore

An animal that only eats meat.

Brood

To sit on a nest of eggs to keep them safe until they hatch.

Cretaceous

The final era of the dinosaurs, 120 to 65 million years ago.

Evolve

The slow process by which animals change over time to adapt to their environment.

Fossil

When something has been fossilised, preserved in rock.

Herbivore

An animal that only eats plants.

Iridescent

Something that shines with different colours when seen from different angles.

MYA

Million years ago.

Nocturnal

When an animal is mostly active during the night.

Omnivore

An animal that eats plants and animals.

Palaeontologist

A scientist who learns about ancient forms of life from fossils.

Piscivore

An animal that only eats fish.

Powered flight

When an animal flaps its wings to propel itself through the air.

Predator

An animal that hunts other animals.

Prey

An animal that is hunted by other animals.

Pterosaur

An extinct group of flying reptiles.

Theropod

A group of dinosaurs that walked on their hind legs.

Elasmosaurus

Alamosaurus

North America

Pacific Ocean

North Atlantic Ocean

South America

South Atlantic Ocean

Earth during the

Cretaceous Period

Parasaurolophus

Pachycephalosaurus

Iguanodon